Meli's Journal

The Forest of Noillid

by

Melissa Anne Poteat

Walk uprightly and harm none.

George W Stevenson

Dedication

At my grandfather's death, memories were found in trunks and boxes that were kept by my grandmother. Her doodles, poems, and letters inspired me to create this series of journals written by Lady Meli. The entire collection of Meli's Journal is dedicated to Walter Clyde Poteat and Florence Elizabeth Frady Poteat

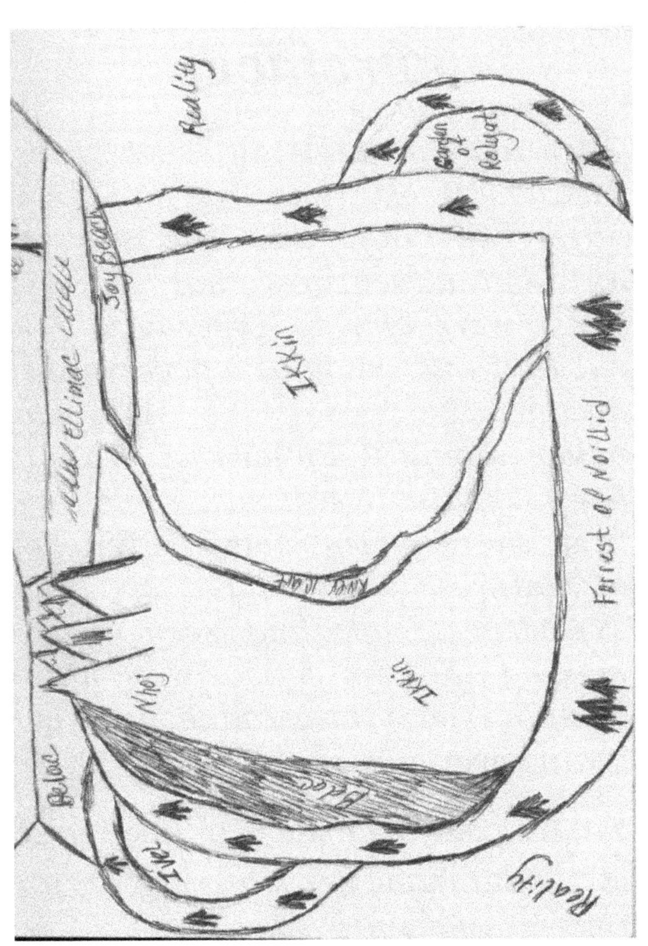
Reality
Garden of Rolyat
Joy Beach
Ikkin
Forrest of Noillid
Nhoj
Ikkin
Belac
Belac
Reality

Preface

Traveling to many different lands, Melinda took time to jot down different things that she saw at different adventures that she and Beast were able to experience. She felt that this would be a good way of documenting what she saw. She never intended anyone of reading her journals. It was just something that she enjoyed doing after her adventures. Writing of her experiences, doodling scenes, and making up poems was a way of her bringing her fantasy lands into her reality world.

Finding out the origins of the Forest of Noillid made her experience with the one who watched over the forest, Noillid, an unforgettable one. Beneath his rough exterior, she *finds that the grouchy little troll would become more to her than she would have ever guessed. He became not only her battle helper; he turned out to be a true friend.*

January

I am not surprised to be in Noillid's forest today. I dreamed of him in my reality sleep last night. I dreamed that underneath his tough exterior there was a kind, gentle and creative little guy. In my dream he was the way he was before he broke the rules and crossed the barriers. He was beautiful and happy. Maybe one day he will see that he is still the same beautiful person on the inside. Until he sees this he will remain cold and harsh.

The first thing noticed in the Forest of Noillid is the smell. The strong scent of pine is both soothing and relaxing. Not like those crazy little pine tree thingies that you hang in *your car; they stink. This is real fresh smelling pine.*

The lush green pines sway to the breeze as if they were dancing slowly to a perfected choreographed piece. It's a beautiful place with pine needled flooring.

February

Today Beast and I were in the Forest of Noillid, but we were at the edge of Belac. This was so cool. We could see them but they could not see us. It was as if the trees acted as an invisible shield.

We watched as the demons in the land rode by on their horses. At first I did not realize that we were invisible so I stood still behind one of the low lying pines. Beast on the other hand was barking and growling, but the demons rode right past us without even noticing.

Walking around the premier of the land, we saw a horrifying sight. The magic in Belac is used for evil only. My heart sank when I saw *innocents brought into the land. My anger got the best of me.*

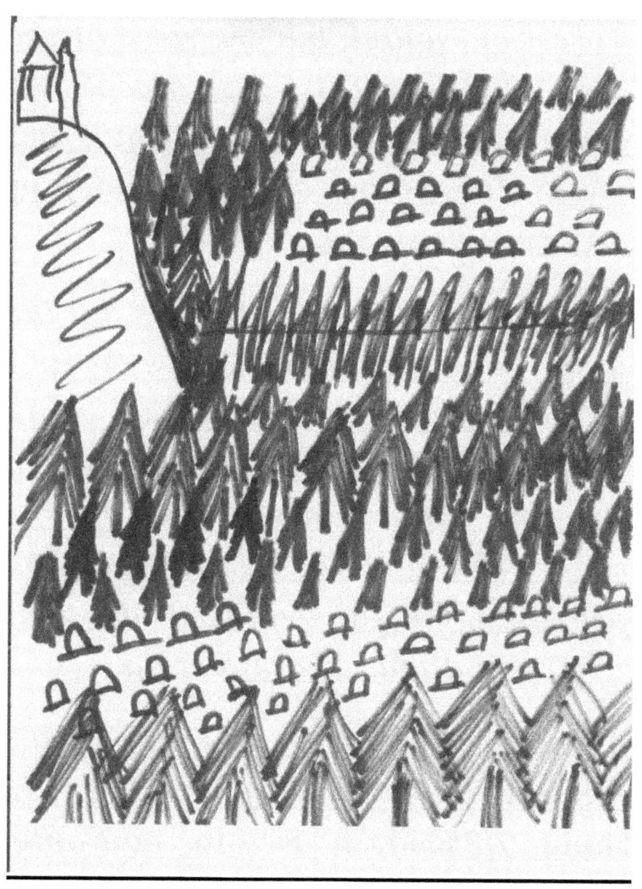

I took three forceful steps towards the edge of the land and hit what felt like a sheet of Plexiglas. I stumbled back holding my nose because it felt like I had broken it. My eyes watered as I reached up and felt the shielded sheet.

This was lesson for me. Whatever land I was in, no matter if I could see the other lands, I could not enter them. I felt defeated. Especially since I could no longer smell the wonderful fragrance from the forest.

March

Today in the forest, Beast and I found out that the trees do things that are not so pretty.

When we entered the forest, we found that the ground was sticky and the pine needles stuck to the bottom of my boots and the bottoms of Beasts' paws. Needless to say it was a sticky mess.

A felt a glop of something hit my head and run down the side of my face. Taking my hand to wipe it off, my hand stuck to my face. Beast yelped when a glop of the sticky substance landed on his back.

Before we knew it, we were being bombarded with these huge globs. I looked up at the tall pines and saw *that the goop was coming from them. It was the sap oozing out of them.*

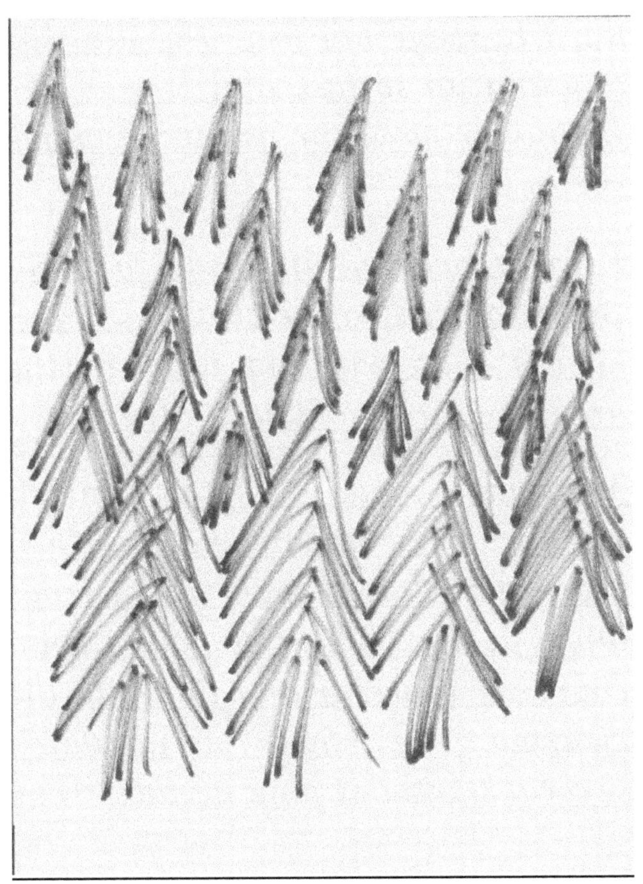

YUCK!

We started to run from the trees when I found that it was getting hard to move my feet. The sap was building up so fast that it was like trying to move in a vat of maple syrup.

I saw a clearing up ahead so I told Beast to head to the clearing. I was hoping that with no trees in the area, the sap would not be there.

We finally made it to the clearing after what seemed like hours. When I looked at Beast I could not help but laugh at him. Where he had fallen a couple of times, trying to get to the clearing, he had accumulated several thousand pine needles. They had stuck to the sap that had fallen on top of him.

Beast did not seem to think it was too funny. After I realized that I too had a gazillion pine needles stuck on me, I did not think that it was too funny.

Then I figured I might as well laugh. When it rains tree sap and you fall into pine needles, you might as well laugh about it.

April

After our last visit to Noillid's forest, I was a little reluctant when I saw that Beast and I had returned.

The ground was not sticky, so I figured that was a good thing; I was wrong.

I don't know why the forest does not like us in it. We did nothing to it except enjoy its wonderful smells and sights. Then it dawned on me just who's forest it was. I asked Beast if he thought that maybe that mischievous Noillid had something to do with the misadventures we were having here.

Just as the words came from my mouth, I was hit in the head with a huge pine cone. Just as the visit before, Beast and I found ourselves dodging falling objects. This time it was the pine cones.

Now these were not your typical pinecones. Some of them were as big as my head, whereas others were regular sized. The regular sized ones were the small ones.

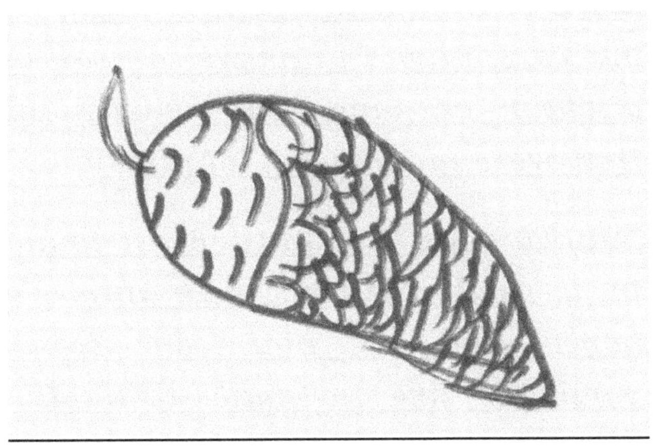

Beast and I looked puzzled at each other. I told him to run. It was as if the skies had opened up with a downpour, only it was the trees and it was pine cones. Maybe a hail storm would be a better example.

It made me think of the hail storm that was in my reality world the day before. The insurance companies were swamped with claims on cars and houses. George and I even had to call in a claim on our cars. I don't think we can call in a claim on pine cone concussions that were incurred in a fantasy.

Anyway, we ran until Beast found us a small cave to duck into. I'd hoped that the pine cone storm would be like the hail storm and pass quickly; it did and not a moment too soon. Just as the pounding of the pine cones stopped, *we realized we were not alone on the small cave. All I could think of was that we had found ourselves in some bear's cave, and I was sure he was not to happy about having company.*

Beast and I ran out of the cave in a panic. I quickly called for my sword as I whirled around expecting to see some huge black or brown bear.

What came out took both me and Beast for surprise. Two little creatures ran out of the cave and took off into the forest. I looked at Beast as he looked at me. I asked him, "What the heck was that?"

I was not sure if they were small dogs, cats, or some other something else. One was black and one was white with black and brown patches. The black one had curly hair and the white one had long hair. I did not get a look at their faces because I believe they were more afraid of us than we were of them.

I am glad that I called for my sword to disappear because as I stepped back to continue our adventure, I stumbled on the many pine cones that were lying on the ground and fell. Beast came over and started licking me in the face. I told him that I was ok and to stop licking me.

This land was really starting to confuse me. Was Noillid behind all of this? Why did the land seem to not want us here? And what the heck came running out of the cave?

May

Today in the forest, I noticed there was a strong perfumy smell. The trees were covered with vines and hanging from the vines was these beautiful groups of light and dark purple flowers.

My nose started to drip and my eyes started burning. Beast started sneezing as he does when he sniffs something up his snout. I rubbed my eyes a couple of times, but that just seemed to make things worse. My vision went blurry so I sat down on the soft pine needles. I had the uncontrollable urge to sleep; so I did.

The sleep I fell into was strange. It was like I was asleep, but a part of me was not. I guess when people *speak of an out of body experience, which was what I was having.*

My essence lifted out of my body. I was standing over my body looking down at it. My body was lying on the bed of pine needles with my head resting on Beast's back. He too was sleeping. I watched as his essence also lifted out of his body.

We started walking around the forest until we found ourselves at the edge of Ikkin. It was a scene that we had been before. The field was full of flowers and Beast and I were running through them. There was the family of deer and me and Beast. With a blip, the scene changed to me and Beast in the village celebrating with the villagers. It was like watching a movie and we were the key actors.

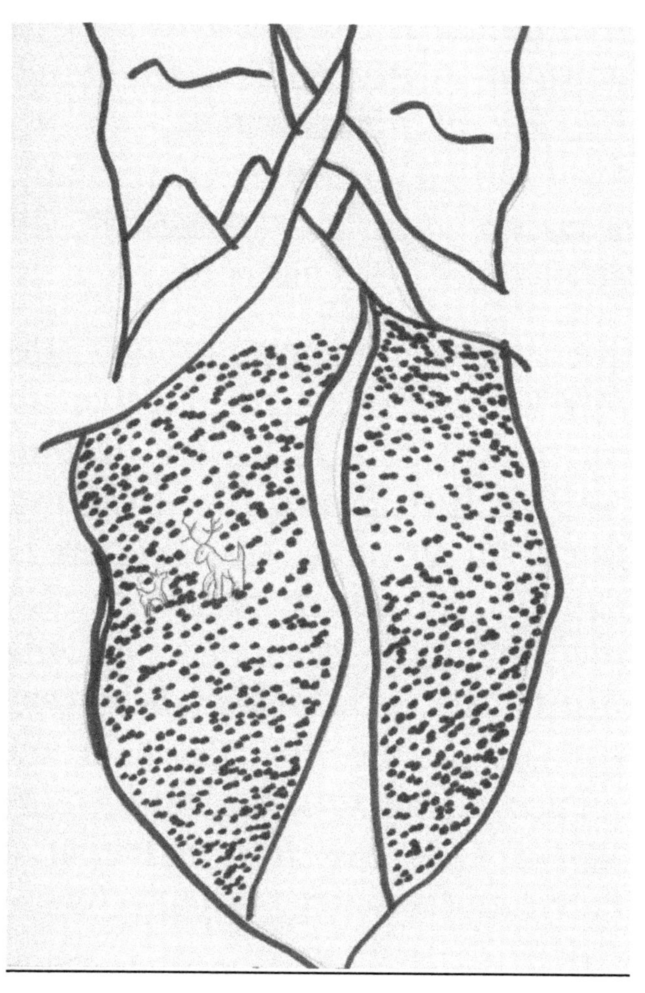

Then I saw Noillid and his leaves. I looked at Beast and started to say something, but no words would come out of my mouth.

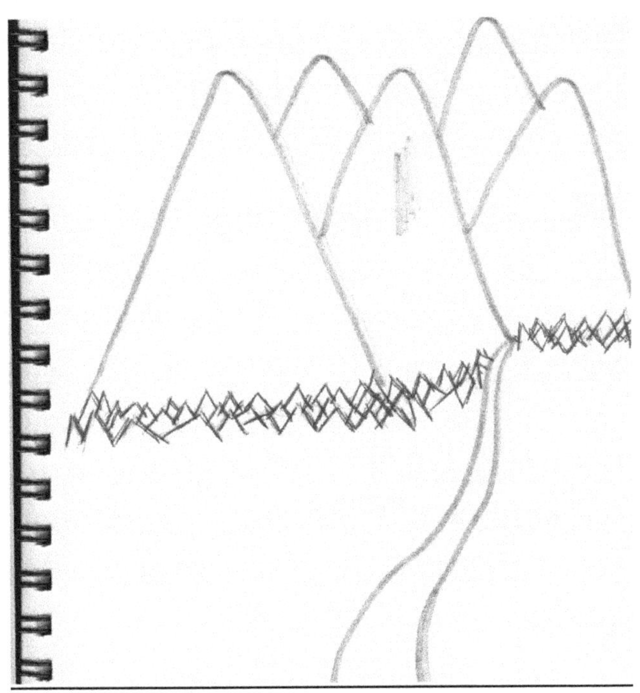

When I looked back towards Ikkin, the land had changed to the mountains of Nhoj. I watched as Beast and I were exploring the rough jagged base of the mountains.

I remembered that day as if it had just happened. I remember wanting to explore the massive peaks from the first day I saw them from Ikkin.

Why was I seeing things that I had already experienced? I was confused as I looked down at Beast. He never looked at me. It was as if he was enjoying a movie. Looking back at the land, I saw Noillid climbing up the side of the mountain. I thought how strange it was seeing him again.

Looking back up, I saw that now we were viewing Ellimac and the wonderful creatures the waters *held. Watching Beast and myself playing around with the whales and dolphins made me miss the wonderful times there.*

I laughed, but no sound was made, when I saw Noillid and his raft. I

was starting to see a connection; Noillid.

The same with Joy Beach, Rolyat, Assilem, and Arreis. Noillid was always there. It was still unclear what happening.

Suddenly I felt something pulling me back towards my body that was still laying on the pine needles. I did not fight the urge to go back.

I felt my essence return to my body and I woke up to a voice asking me if I was alright. I opened my eyes to find that Noillid was bent down beside of me. He told me that the wisteria vine had over powered my senses. He took me and Beast to his dwelling in the middle of the forest where he gave us something to drink and eat.

June

I had hoped that this visit to the forest would be a peaceful one. Noillid was very hospitable the last visit and after talking with him, I knew he was not the reason Beast and I had not had good experiences in his forest.

He did not need to explain the dream to me because I had seen the lands through his eye. I saw how he looks on at the other lands and the creatures in it and how he does not get to join in the celebrations.

He does have this wonderful forest, but the sacrifices he went through, I am sure he would never have crossed the threshold of Ikkin if only he had known the price of eternal loneliness and un-acceptance.

Walking through the lush pines, I felt sad for him. He is not one that wishes for sympathy, oh no. He would rather have a pine needle put into one of his eyes rather than someone fell sorry for him. He told me that, but I still can't help but wish that things were a bit different for him. Getting to understand him a little better helps me to accept him more for who he is and what he has been through.

I guess the old saying is true. You should never think badly of someone. Until you have walked a mile in their shoes, you do not know what they have been through.

July

Today in the forest there was a light feeling; a feeling of hope and life. The treetops revealed why.

I had noticed that there were like spider webs on the trees both high and low. I did not realize they were actually cocoons. This I realized as they started bursting open and beautiful butterflies sprang from them.

Thousands of beautifully colored winged insects flew high above the tree tops. There were so many, they covered the once bright blue sky, causing darkness to fall over the forest until they flew away. Another batch hatched causing the same effect. This continued several

times. I asked Beast how in the world did the cocoons keep producing so many. Of course he did not have and answer for me.

August

Today Beast and I were met by the two strange looking creatures in the forest. They went scurrying by us just as we stepped into the pine needled covered land.

I told Beast I had an idea. If we captured the creatures, I think they would be good company for Noillid. I called for a snack. A peanut butter sandwich appeared in my hand. Beast went crazy; he loves peanut butter sandwiches. I sat down in the pine needles and tore the sandwich in half. I handed half to Beast and I munched on the other half. I kept saying how good it was, along with smacking my lips as I ate it. Beast wolfed his down as usual, but this actually helped with the effect.

Before long, the two little creatures' curiosity got the best of them, which I knew it would.

Slowly they came out of the low lying pines curious to see what we were eating.

I called for another sandwich and it appeared in my hand. Once again I tore the sandwich in half only this time, when I handed Beast his, the other half I tore again and held the pieces out towards the little guys.

It took a while, but slowly they inched to me and took the morsels with their mouths. They sat with us and enjoyed their snacks. I told them that I knew of someone who would take care of them and they would not have to live out in the forest by themselves. Although I had not spoken with Noillid about having guests, I just felt this was the right thing to do.

Now that I had won the creatures over, I had to take them to Noillid and get him to agree. I was going to have to make Noillid believe it was his idea, but being a woman I felt I had the ability to do this. After all, I am Lady Meli.

I took the strange looking creatures to Noillid's dwelling. He was there working; piddling I should say. I told him that I had found the little guys wondering around in the forest and they needed taking care of. At first he was argumentative and saying they were wild creatures and they could take care of themselves but I insisted that they were too small to be out in the forest by themselves and they needed someone to take care of them. I told him that I thought the names Yhprum and Ronnoc seemed like good things to call them.

"Oh no," he grumbled. "Don't name them.

He mumbled something about having to take care of everything and then I said, "Please".

I don't know if it was my plead that got him or the fact that the little guys were so cute and were sitting at his feet with pitiful eyes as if they were begging also, but he finally agreed to let them stay with him and he promised me that he would take care of them. He said after all I had already named them and it would be shameful to have names and not have someone around to *call them by their names. Whatever his logic was, I was just happy he agreed to let them hang out with him.*

I felt so good in my return to reality. I found a home for two of the cutest little creatures; so strange looking they were cute, and I found a couple of friends to hang out with Noillid.

September

Many times when Beast and I entered Noillid's forest, I would hear an owl hiding in the trees. His hoo-hoot's were loud so that's how I knew he was there.

Today was a bit different. Instead of the normal hoo-hoot, I heard "Me-Meli". Now this freaked me out a bit. In reality there is an old wives tale that says if a screech owl says your name, you or someone with that name will die soon. I was hoping in fantasy old wives tales did not exist.

As we strolled through the sweet pine smelling evergreen, we came upon a patch of low lying green ferns. It was a beautiful and peaceful place. Beast and I decided to sit for a spell and have a picnic.

We figured we would just have a nice peaceful afternoon, and hope that nothing crazy would happen.

Going to so many lands and having so many battles, sometimes you have to make time to just relax. I heard in a movie once this was called copasquaching; which simple means sitting and reflecting on life. So we were copasquaching.

Sitting in the ferns, I called for a special treat for Beast; a chew bone, and a cigarette for me. I had leaned up against a fallen tree and sat and watched Beast enjoy his bone.

The thing about copasquaching is that you forget about your surroundings, therefore I did not see the snake that had slithered up on *the log that I was leaned up against. I did however hear that owl say "Me-Meli". I thought to myself that he was starting to get a bit annoying.*

Suddenly I heard a loud screech from behind me. I glance up in the direction it was coming and I saw this huge owl flying right at me. Seeing that he was not going to stop, I ducked down. As the owl flew over my head, I felt something hit my shoulder. Looking up at the giant bird, I saw that he had a long black snake hanging out of his mouth. I realized it was a large snake.

The owl and the snake battled in the air until finally the snake turned into black goo. It burst into blue glittery smoke and floated into the air. The owl then turned and soared back towards me only this time he landed on the log that was supporting my back.

The owl gave me a hoo-hoot and then spoke. He told me that the snake was getting ready to strike me in the back. I told the owl thank-you and asked him if there was some way I could repay him for his courageous deed. He looked towards Beast's bone. I thought it a bit strange that an owl would like a chewy bone, but I called for another bone and handed it to him. He sat on the log and sharpened his beak on the rawhide bone while Beast chewed on his, and I finished my cigarette.

You never know what is going to happen from day-to-day no matter if you are in fantasy or reality.

October

Today was a busy day. Beast and I had to run to the bank for George, pay a couple of bills, go to Wal-Mart and pick up trick-or-treat candies for the visiting goblins tonight, wash the car, and carve the pumpkin for the front porch. Needless to say Beast and I entered the forest a bit late. That was not a bad thing though. We found ourselves at Noillid's dwelling where he and his two little friends were enjoying a nice fire.

There was a nip in the air so the fire was a nice welcoming. Noillid had three roasted rabbits on a stick and the three were getting ready to eat a bite of supper. He offered me and Beast one but I told him that we had *just eaten. He thought I might think bad of him for killing the rabbits, but I told him that killing for food and clothing was not bad and I*

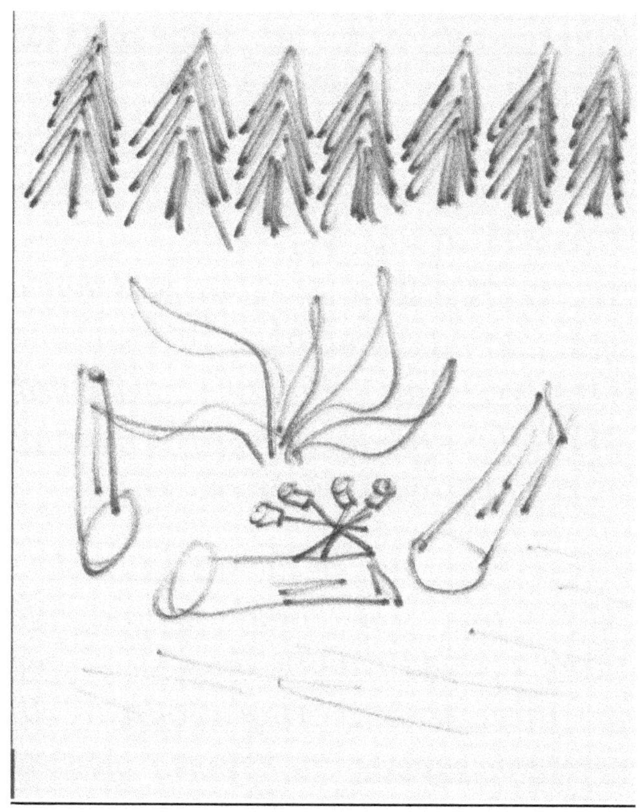

thought nothing about it. I told him my favorite food was steak which came from a cow. He informed me that cow was not a wild animal. I agreed with him but I told him that in reality cows were raised for milk, butter, cheese, and meat; and sometimes clothing. He thought of it as a little strange that in reality we don't have to hunt our food like he does. I told him of our hunters called Ingles, Food Lion, and BI-LO. He said that they were strange names for hunters. It seemed a bit confusing to him so I just let him know that hunting and killing was fine when it meant survival; not when it meant for keeping souls in Belac. Beast and I did enjoy some of the blue glittery wine he had gotten from the garden of Rolyat.

When the three had finished their rabbits, I called for a wonderful treat from the great hunter Wal-Mart. It was a bag of marshmallows. I gathered a couple of sticks from a nearby tree and placed several marshmallows on them and held them over the roaring fire. Once the marshmallows were black and brown toasted I handed one of the sticks to Noillid. He was very curious at this strange looking treat. I took one off of my stick and gave it to Beast; he loves toasted marshmallows. Then I handed one each to Yhprum and Ronnoc.

After tasting the toasted treat, Noillid asked me where the marshmallows grew. I told him at the marshmallow factory. This conversation took a while, but we enjoyed toasting and eating and talking about reality and the strange things that went on there like manufacturing and processes. One day I will let him in on automobiles and air planes. I did not feel he was ready for that yet.

November

George had an out of town business meeting tonight so I told Beast we would enter fantasy late and maybe just spend the night there as long as it was not in Belac. I was very happy to see that it was not; instead we were in the middle of Noillid's forest with bright stars in the night sky.

I called for a couple of blankets to put on the pine needle ground. I was happy to see a bear skin appear on the ground with a rabbit skin over blanket on top of it. Beast ran onto the blankets and rolled around on them.

That crazy dog, he is such a lush at times.

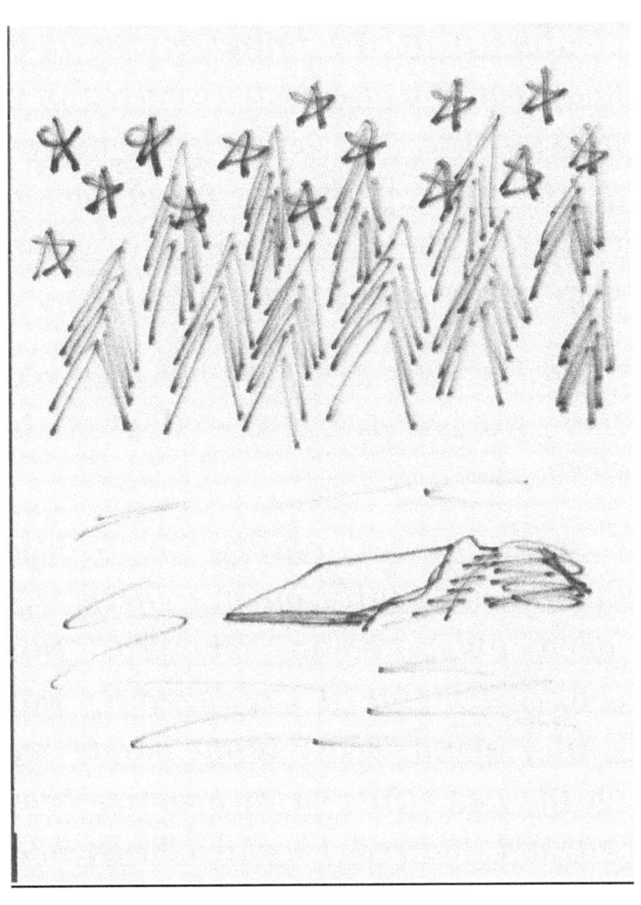

Looking up at the starry sky, I watched as they danced their nightly dance for me. I felt

comforted at the sound of the hoo-hoot from the owl that I spotted in a nearby tree. His yellow eyes glowed as the light of the big bright moon reflected them. I knew with him near, Beast and I would be safe.

With the total relaxation I received from the forest, I soon drifted off to sleep.

I woke up in reality to George kissing me gently on my cheek. He joked about being replaced. This confused me until I realized he was joking about Beast lying beside me on the bed. This was a practice that was not allowed. I scolded Beast in a joking tone about him knowing better. They both knew I was full of it.

December

Entering into the forest today, the first thing noticed was the cold. I quickly called for a jacked; which a hooded brown leather cloak wrapped around me. Beast seemed to enjoy the cold since he had already grown his winter coat in reality.

There was snow on the ground and the snow was still falling. The forest was quiet. People say you can't hear it snow, but when things are so quiet you can. All that could be heard was the crunch of the snow beneath our feet and the gentle laying of snow flakes on the land.

Breathing in the cold air was like receiving a burst of refreshment into my lungs.

We walked passed the different lands and watched as they too were enjoying the beautiful white snow. Even Joy Beach looked wintery with its white sands covered in even whiter snow.

Checking in on Noillid, we knocked on his door. We were greeted by the little fellow and his two friends. He welcomed us into his small home and gave us some hot chocolate from the River Icart along with some sugar cookies he had gathered from the fields of Ikkin. We had a nice visit but like always I had to return to reality.

In your forest of green
Pine scented and clean
I found new adventures
New creatures and things.

New ways of seeing
My lands of fantasy
New admirations
Of my friend of green.

Noillid's forest
I can't wait to return
To re-experience the many
Things I have learned.

The true storyteller...Uncle George

www.ingramcontent.com/pod-product-compliance
Ingram Content Group UK Ltd.
Pitfield, Milton Keynes, MK11 3LW, UK
UKHW020217250726
13967UKWH00001B/47

9 781105 715167